A Gift For:

_____

From:

_____

Published by Hallmark Gift Books,
a division of Hallmark Cards, Inc.,
Kansas City, MO 64141
Visit us on the Web at Hallmark.com.

Editorial Director: Delia Berrigan
Editor: Kim Schworm Acosta
Art Director: Chris Opheim
Designer: Brian Pilachowski
Production Designer: Dan Horton

ISBN: 978-1-63059-739-9
1XKT2334

Made in China
0718

Snow Letter Left Behind

![Hallmark]

A STORY FROM THE HALLMARK HOLIDAY SERIES
Written by Keely Chace   Illustrated by Mike Esberg

'Twas the very last pickup for holiday mail,
when someone came calling last minute:
"Wait, Mr. Postman! Please open your bag.
This letter just has to go in it!"

The postman was happy to pick up one more,
and he gave his on-time guarantee.
(Sadly, the letter slipped out of his bag,
and nobody happened to see!)

The poor little letter! Left out in the cold!
Would it lie there forever and freeze?
Snow way! In a twinkling, it fluttered and flew
on the *whoosh* of a crisp winter breeze.

It looped through the air, and it landed with care
on a freshly cut tree gliding past.
It kept right on riding until it arrived
by a snow-sprinkled cabin at last.

A welcoming neighbor was waiting outside
with a plate full of cookies—oh, yum!
In all the excitement, the letter filled in
as a napkin to catch cookie crumbs!

The letter was sweeter and sprinklier now,
which attracted a little red friend.
Wheee! The bird snatched it and took to the sky.
Hooray! It was moving again!

The bird flew it swiftly to Snow Central Park,
and she let it drop lazily down.
It fell on a bench seat, its journey all done . . .
unless it could somehow get found!

Santa
North Pole

Well, somebody found the lost letter all right,
when he sat down to snack on a nut.
He rested a spell and then stood up to go
with the letter stuck right to his . . . *pants.*

This gentleman went on his way, unaware,
just a-smiling and tipping his hat.
Finally, a friendly dog snatched it away—
'cause no message should travel like that!

The dog took it quickly and dashed to a spot
where a cool group was jamming along.
The letter picked up on their wintry groove,
riding high on the notes of their song!

From there, it danced on to a magical place
full of all kinds of fun things to try.
It bounced on a seesaw—a snowgirl did, too . . .
and she shot it right into the sky!

Higher and higher it climbed 'til it came

to a marvelous hot-air balloon.

Here was a great way to travel—yippee!

With some luck, it would reach Santa soon!

Oops! Before long, things began to look wrong.

They'd been heading in quite the wrong way.

It seemed like all hope of delivery was doomed . . .

. . .'til they passed by a north-going sleigh!

The boy and his sleigh gladly took it aboard,
and they put on a flying display!
They rocketed north, and at last it appeared
that the letter was well on its way.

Then, sure enough, the North Pole came in view
like a peppermint stick up ahead!
The letter swooped downward to make the last push
with some friends zooming by on their sled.

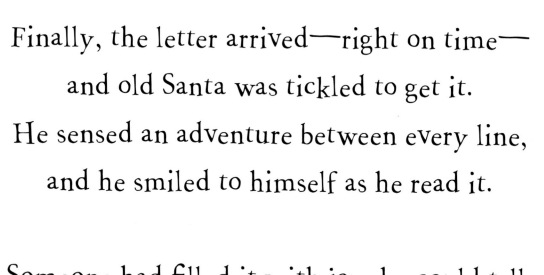

Finally, the letter arrived—right on time—
and old Santa was tickled to get it.
He sensed an adventure between every line,
and he smiled to himself as he read it.

Someone had filled it with joy, he could tell.
Someone had written with care.
Just goes to show, with some magic and love,
Santa's letters will always get there!

If this chilly adventure warmed your heart,
or if perhaps you just liked the art,
we would love to hear from you.

Please write a review at Hallmark.com,
e-mail us at booknotes@hallmark.com,
or send your comments to:

Hallmark Book Feedback
P.O. Box 419034
Mail Drop 100
Kansas City, MO 64141